The Kingdom *of* Little Wounds